LITTLE RED RIDING HOOD

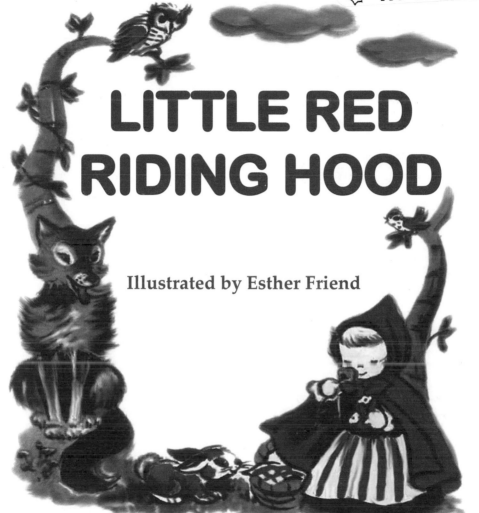

Illustrated by Esther Friend

Published by

THE TOON STUDIO

OF BEVERLY HILLS

ONCE upon a time there was a little village girl who was as sweet as sugar and as good as bread.

Her mother loved her very much, and her grandmother was even fonder of her. This kind grandmother had made her a pretty red cloak with a hood, in which the child looked so bright and gay that everyone called her Little Red Riding-Hood.

One day her mother made some cakes and said to her: "Go, my child, and see how your

grandmother is. I hear she has
been ill. Take her one of these
cakes and this little pot of butter."

So Little Red Riding-Hood set
out at once. As she walked
through the woods she met a big
wolf. He would have gobbled her

up then and there, but some
woodcutters were near by and
he did not dare. But he did ask
her where she was going.

"I am going to my grandmother."
"Does she live far off?" asked the
wolf.

"Oh, yes," answered Little Red Riding-Hood. "She lives beyond the mill you see way down there, at the first house in the village."

"All right," said the wolf. "I'll go and visit her too. I will take this way, and we'll see who gets there first."

Soon the wolf arrived at the grandmother's cottage and knocked at the door - *tap! tap!*

"Who is there?"

"It is your own Little Red Riding-Hood," said the wolf, making his voice sound as much like Little Red Riding-Hood's as he could.

The good old woman, who wasn't feeling well and so was in bed, called out: "Pull the string, my dear, and the latch will fly up."

The wolf pulled the string and the door opened. He sprang upon the poor old grandmother

and swallowed her all in one gulp, for it was more than three days since he had had a bite. He did not feel very well after that, but he shut the door, put on the grandmother's cap, and stretched himself out in the old woman's bcd to wait for Little Red Riding-Hood.

By and by Little Red Riding-Hood came knocking at the cottage door - *tap! tap!*

"Who is there?"

At first Little Red Riding-Hood was frightened at the hoarse voice of the wolf. But she made up her mind that her grandmother must have a cold.

"It is your own Little Red Riding-
Hood," she answered. "I have
brought you a cake and a little pot
of butter which Mother had made
and sent you."

Then the wolf called out, softening
his voice as well as he could: "Pull

the string, my dear, and the latch will fly up."

Little Red Riding-Hood pulled the string and the door opened. When the wolf saw her come in, he hid himself under the bedclothes and said:

"Put the cake and the little pot of butter on the shelf, and come here." And so Little Red Riding-Hood put the cake and butter on the shelf and went over to the wolf. She was very much surprised to see how

strange her Grandmother looked in her night clothes and said:
"Grandmother, what great arms you have!"
"The better to hug you, my child!"

"Grandmother, what great ears you have!"

"The better to hear you, my child!"

"Grandmother, what great eyes you have!"

"The better to see you, my child!"

"Grandmother, what great teeth you have!"

"The better to eat you!"

With these words the wicked wolf fell upon poor Little Red Riding-Hood.

And there the story ends. Nobody knows just what happened. Some say that the woodsmen were so near by, cutting trees, that they heard Little Red Riding-Hood scream and came running, just in time to save her. And they say, too, that when the woodsmen cut the wolf open, there they found the grandmother, whole and sound!